Friends and Pals and Brothers, Too

Friends and Pals and Brothers, Too

by Sarah Wilson

illustrated by Leo Landry

Henry Holt and Company ☆ New York

Henry Holt and Company, LLC
Publishers since 1866
175 Fifth Avenue
New York, New York 10010
www.HenryHoltKids.com

Library of Congress Cataloging-in-Publication Data
Wilson, Sarah.
Friends and pals and brothers, too / Sarah Wilson ; illustrated by Leo Landry.—1st ed.
p.   cm.
Summary: Two brothers who are best friends have fun together throughout the year.
ISBN-13: 978-0-8050-7643-1 / ISBN-10: 0-8050-7643-3
[1. Brothers—Fiction. 2. Friendship—Fiction. 3. Seasons—Fiction. 4. Stories in rhyme.]
I. Landry, Leo, ill. II. Title.   PZ8.3.W698Fri 2008   [E]—dc22   2007002829

First Edition—2008 / Designed by Amelia May Anderson
The artist used watercolor and pencil to create the illustrations for this book.
Printed in the United States of America on acid-free paper. ∞
1 3 5 7 9 10 8 6 4 2

For Anna Barrett, author of the Neecie books,
with admiration and delight

—S. W.

For my Children's Book Shop friends and pals

—L. L.

My brother's short with stompy feet.

I'm tall, not small. I like to eat.

Our shirts hang loose. Our socks are bright.
We tell ourselves we look just right.

I call him Squirrel. He calls me Bear.

We sing in bed. We mud our hair.

We hang our shoes outside on trees.

We like to snack on cakes and cheese.

In fall we go on nature hikes.

We beat on drums. We ride our bikes.

We jump in leaves. We shout. We rake.

We pumpkin paint. We pancake bake.

In wintertime we're acrobats.

We roll in snow. We wear strange hats.

We ski. We slide. We make up jokes.

We slurp hot soup. We sleep in coats.

In spring we bring out balls and bats.

We look for frogs. We pet strange cats.

We puddle jump. We swing from bars.

We make up shapes in clouds and stars.

In summertime we jump from docks.

We spit out pits. We skip small rocks.

We roll on grass. We chase. We hide.

We pitch our tents and sleep outside.

The whole year long we're always there
With ketchup-ed bread and jam to share.

I'm Bear. He's Squirrel. We stick like glue.
We're friends. We're pals. Forever, too.